Maisie Bites the Big Apple

E

Maisie
Manhattan
Mystery *
Mayhem

Maisie Bites
the Big Apple

Author and illustrator Aileen Paterson

GLOWWORM BOOKS

For the Children of New York

Many thanks to Alison McGachy of
The John Muir Trust for her help with reference material

Thank you, too, to my neighbour Eveline Nicholson

Thanks to Mark Blackadder

© Aileen Paterson

First Published in 2002 by
Glowworm Books Ltd. Unit 7, Greendykes Industrial Estate,
Broxburn, West Lothian, EH52 6PG, Scotland

Telephone: 01506-857570
Fax: 01506-858100
URL: http://www.glowwormbooks.co.uk

ISBN 1 871512 69 7

Designed by Mark Blackadder

Reprint Code   10   9   8   7   6   5   4   3   2   1

Other Maisie titles in the Series:

A big yellow taxi was whizzing along busy streets with a cabful of cats and one blue budgie. Clouds of steam puffed out of the ground and huge buildings reached up to the sky. Maisie Mackenzie was one of the cats. She was off on her travels again, far from Morningside.

She was in NEW YORK.

Her latest trip had begun a few days ago, back home in Edinburgh. She and Granny had gone shopping with their posh pernickety neighbour, Mrs McKitty, and her niece, Lydia. Mrs McKitty had news for everyone. They were all going to America! On Tuesday! ! !

"I'm sure you remember my cousin Griselda, the FAMOUS Opera Star."

(Maisie and Granny remembered her very well. On her visit to Edinburgh she had sung to them. Her voice was louder than a hundred bagpipes.)

"Well dears," continued Mrs McKitty, "Griselda has invited us to her Opening Night in The Big Apple. She's even sent a ticket for my budgie."

"She's going to sing inside a big apple?" Maisie was amazed.

"Silly you, The Big Apple is another name for New York," piped up Lydia, who knew almost everything.

Granny was flabbergasted. "America on Tuesday? Opera? It's very kind . . . but I don't think . . .er . . .er . . .er."

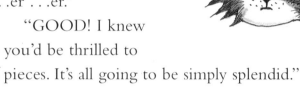
"GOOD! I knew you'd be thrilled to pieces. It's all going to be simply splendid."

SO THAT WAS THAT.

And now they had arrived in New York.

Maisie's nose sniffed adventure in the air. What an exciting place!

At last they reached the hotel where Mrs McKitty's famous cousin was waiting for them. When they got out of the lift at the 92nd floor, Maisie noticed three cats with fancy hats walking behind them. Next moment they had vanished into thin air, but there was no time for thinking about vanishing cats. A door opened wide and there stood Madam Griselda Tremolo. A large marmalade cat wearing a large sparkling green necklace.

"WELCOME, welcome, my darling Scottywotties! How lovely to see you all again."

There was a lot of hugging and she swooped down on Maisie. "Special kissywissies for you, dearest Lydia's little friend." Billy the budgie flew out of the way in case he was next!

As soon as she could, Maisie escaped from the hugging and unpacking and set off to explore and discover things. She discovered that there were lots of rooms and lots of pictures of Madam Griselda.

She also discovered a tall cat. He was wearing a black jacket and striped trousers and he looked very important.

"Hello," she said. "My name is Maisie. I think you must be Mister Tremolo."

"I think not, Miss Maisie. My name is Hoots. I am Madam's butler." "I see," said Maisie, who didn't see at all. "Is butling hard work?"

"Absolutely! I am in charge of everything AND I have to guard Madam's necklace . . .

The Verdi Emeralds. It is worth three million dollars. Quite valuable, you see."

"Absolutely!" cried Maisie.

Three million dollars! She couldn't wait to tell Granny and Billy about Hoots and the necklace, but Mrs McKitty had much more interesting news for them.

"I've asked Griselda to sing for us this evening. It will be such a treat. I love a bit of culture."

"And I'm going to play the piano for Auntie Griselda," said Lydia, the most cultured kitten in Lady Road.

"She's a dab hand with the scherzos and arpeggios," purred Mrs McKitty. "Maisie could learn a lot from Lydia."

After dinner, the musical evening began . . .

Oh dear. Madam Griselda's voice was just as powerful and noisy as Maisie remembered. The windows rattled! The walls shook! The high notes made her ears POP! Mrs McKitty was in Seventh Heaven. The others couldn't wait for it to end. Maisie was glad when it was time for bed.

Granny kissed her goodnight, then she curled up with her favourite detective story, 'Inspector Clevercloggs and The Cat Burglar'. Inspector Clevercloggs was very clever indeed. He always solved each mystery before the end of the book! She soon forgot about the musical evening.

Next day, Madam Griselda had another treat for her visitors. Not another sing-song. They were off to do some sightseeing. 'Superduper!' thought Maisie. She was disappointed to find that Lydia wanted to visit museums. Maisie thought that might be boring, but she was in for a surprise . . . or two.

In the morning they visited a museum filled with dinosaurs. Lydia told everyone lots of fossil facts. Mrs McKitty told everyone that one of the dinosaurs looked just like her friend, Miss Gingersnapp! Suddenly, Maisie noticed three cats watching them.

The same cats with hats she'd seen at the hotel. When they saw Maisie watching them . . . they vanished AGAIN. It was very odd.

In the afternoon they went to another museum. It was the funniest building Maisie had ever seen. It looked just like Mrs McKitty's hat.

Inside there were lots of paintings just like the ones Maisie did at school. Some of them were very strange . . . but not as strange as the vanishing cats. They were there too and once again, when they saw Maisie watching . . . they vanished.

Her whiskers tingled. She hadn't read twelve books about Inspector Clevercloggs for nothing. Something fishy was going on. She told Hoots that she thought the mysterious cats were crooks, trying to get their paws on Madam Griselda's necklace. The only trouble was that no one else had seen them.

"I think you must be imagining things Miss Maisie," laughed the butler. "If there were any rascals about I would notice immediately. Madam calls me Eagle-Eye Hoots!"

That evening everyone teased Maisie about the cats that weren't there.

Billy said she was a daft scone. Lydia said she had been reading too many silly detective stories. Maisie said Lydia was a nincompoop!

Poor Maisie.

But Maisie wasn't imagining things. The three cats were real.

Salami Sam, Awful Orville & Dainty Dexter

They were known to New York policecats as The Macaroni Gang. There was Awful Orville, Dainty Dexter and, their leader, Salami Sam. Awful Orville loved being awful. Dainty Dexter loved cookies. He kept them in his violin case. Salami Sam loved expensive jewels.

So far, he hadn't managed to snatch The Verdi Emeralds, but he wasn't going to stop trying.

AT LAST, the Opening Night of the Opera arrived.

'MIMI CAMELLIA'
starring Madam Griselda Tremolo
and Roberto Fandango,
the big noise from Napoli

Mrs McKitty and Lydia were very excited. The others weren't quite so excited. Billy liked Jazz, Granny liked Pipe Bands and Maisie was feeling gloomy. She was even more gloomy when Lydia told them that all Operas have unhappy endings. Granny put some hankies in her handbag.

When they got to the Opera House they went to Madam Griselda's dressing room to wish her luck. Then they took their seats. A few minutes later, the red velvet curtains opened wide and the show began . . .

    The stage was filled with cats. The orchestra began to play.
Griselda and Roberto began to sing – and they didn't stop until
the interval!

After the interval, things were different . . .

Madam Griselda (MIMI) was all alone on the stage. She looked sad and she seemed to be unwell. She was lying on a sofa, wearing a nightdress. She coughed once or twice, but she was still singing as loudly as ever.

Suddenly Maisie heard whispering from the row in front.

Helpmabob!

The three cats and their fancy hats were there! She leaned forward to listen to what they were saying. "Gee Boss," whispered Dainty Dexter, "Dis is a sad story. Things don't look good. The fat lady is sick."

"Yeah," whispered Awful Orville. "What's more, the fat lady ain't wearing the necklace."

"Jumping jackrabbits! Let's go!" whispered Salami Sam. "Now's our chance!"

 Maisie wasn't feeling gloomy now. She knew where the necklace might be and she had to get there before The Macaroni Gang. Lydia was very angry when Maisie rushed off, followed by Billy.

But the others didn't notice.

Granny, Mrs McKitty and Hoots were fast asleep!

"Where are we going?" asked Billy, who had no idea what Maisie was up to.

"Follow me and you will see," she said as she ran downstairs.

When she got to Madam Griselda's dressing room she found it unlocked. There lay the necklace, unguarded. She grabbed it and ran. The Macaroni Gang arrived just too late to steal their prize, but just in time to see Maisie running off with it.

They charged after her, yowling and growling, and at last Billy saw the vanishing cats. Maisie had been right after all.

They looked very scary and very angry.

"I'll go and fetch the Police," he squawked. "Don't let them catch you!"

Billy flew off into the night sky and Maisie was on her own, trying to escape from danger. She dived into the Powder Room and hid. It was terrifying when the gang came in and looked around, but they didn't see her behind the door.

She crept out and began running again, but she could hear pawsteps behind her. She found another hiding place in a storeroom full of costumes. Once again they nearly found her and, once again, she managed to escape.

Meanwhile, Billy had managed to find two policecats in Grand Central Station. When he told them his story they jumped into their car and headed for the Opera House . . .

Maisie was still on the run, in the dark, somewhere in the theatre. The three cats were getting nearer and nearer. She saw a door, opened it and kept running, but now she found herself in a blaze of bright light.

SHE WAS ON THE STAGE! IN THE MIDDLE OF THE
OPERA!!

Madam Griselda was horrified and Roberto Fandango was
furious. "Gattina Stupida!" he cried. The audience gasped. This was
much more exciting than 'MIMI CAMELLIA'! Lydia woke up
Mrs McKitty and Granny.

"Look! That stupid Maisie has ruined everything!"

But by now everyone could see that Maisie had the necklace in her paws . . . and behind her were three nasty cats . . . and behind them was Billy . . . and behind Billy there were two police officers!

It was over in a moment. The cops rushed forward and arrested The Macaroni Gang. (When they put pawcuffs on Salami Sam he was not a happy cat.) Madam Griselda got her necklace back and Maisie got lots of kissywissies. The audience stood up and cheered. Granny joined in the cheering, but Mrs McKitty and Lydia were very quiet. So was Eagle-Eye Hoots . . . he was still fast asleep!

Operas have unhappy endings, but Maisie stories always have happy endings.

Next day, Maisie was the toast of New York. She had bitten The Big Apple and it tasted good.

Tootaloothenoo!

Glossary

Budgie	Budgerigar
Morningside	a suburb in Edinburgh
Pernickety	fussy
Lady Road	an Edinburgh road
A dab hand	an expert
Nincompoop	a silly person
Helpmabob!	expression of Scottish surprise
Gattina Stupida	stupid kitten
Tootaloothenoo	Scottish goodbye